Turtle set off very early. He had a long way to go.

As Turtle hurried beneath Cheetah's tree, Cheetah called, "I'm going to get you!"

"Not now," said Turtle. "I'm busy."

"I'll get you later then," yawned Cheetah.

Then Cheetah opened an eye.

"He lived there when he was a tadpole," said Turtle.

"He said it's got everything you could ever want."
Cheetah opened another eye.

"Hey! That sounds like heaven," said Cheetah. "Turtle – I'm coming too!"

"Sorry," said Turtle, "but you're just not fast enough."

"Are you kidding me?" laughed Cheetah. "I'm King of Speed! "

"I haven't time for all this cheetah-chatter," said Turtle. "Us fast ones must get on."

"FAST?" sneered Cheetah. "I'll show you FAST!"
"OK," smiled crafty Turtle. "Show me fast.

Take me over the mountain to
the second tree on the grassy
plain."
Cheetah grabbed Turtle and
vroomed off.

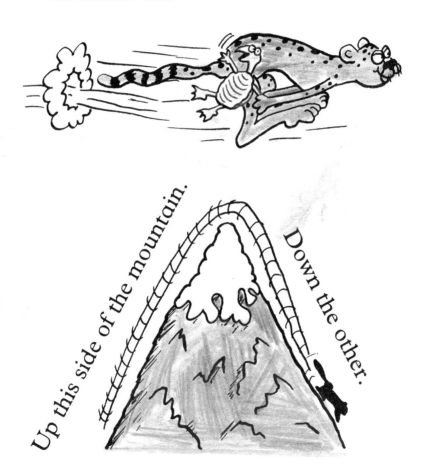

All the way to the second tree on the grassy plain.

"This is easier than walking," thought Turtle.

"First one to touch the tree's the winner!" yelled Turtle.

But Cheetah couldn't answer. "Thank you very much for showing me FAST, Cheetah," said Turtle. "Must dash now. See you!"

"You'll see me all right!" thought Cheetah. "Just wait till I get my breath back ... and my legs are working again!"

Turtle tottered on. He still had a long way to go. Way across the hot, grassy plains.

"Take it easy, little Turtle," said Elephant. "What's the hurry?"

"I'm off to this fantastic place Old Frog told me about," said Turtle. "It has everything you could ever want."

"Like lots of splishy-splashy water and cool oozy mud to roll in?" asked Elephant.

"Yep!" smiled crafty Turtle.

He could see how Elephant could help him.

"That sounds like heaven to me," she sighed. "I'll come with you."
"Sorry, Elephant," said Turtle. "But you're just not big enough."
"Am I going deaf? Or do you need glasses?" asked Elephant. Turtle peered up at her.

"Come closer," said Turtle.
"Left a bit.
Two more steps.
One more big one, please.
That's it."

Turtle looked up at Elephant's
fat tum and said, "Yes – you are
QUITE big. OK. You can come
with me."

And beneath the hot sun they crossed the grassy plain.

"How much further, Turtle?" asked Elephant. "My back feels like it's on fire."

"Sun doesn't bother me," smiled Turtle. "Us big ones can take the heat."

And it's nice and shady under here!

At last they reached the cool jungle.

"Oo-oo-oo," groaned Elephant, as she dropped beneath the shady trees.

Turtle - could you fetch some damp leaves for my poor back?

Turtle fetched the leaves.

"Thank you for showing me how big you are, Elephant," he said. "Got to dash now. See you!"
"You'll see me, Turtle," groaned Elephant.
"Just you wait – till I'm on my feet again!"

And Turtle tottered on ...
... just as Cheetah got his breath
back and his legs working again.
But Turtle still had a long way
to go – through the jungle.
And now he was stuck.

Blinking roots!

"What are you doing?" asked
Chimp.
"Heading for the other side of
the jungle," said Turtle.

"You won't get far," said Chimp. "You're doing it all wrong. Watch me."
He swung from tree to tree.

"I think you need long hairy arms and legs for that," shouted Turtle. "Do you know anyone like that? Someone to swing me through the jungle?"

"There's my brother," yelled
Chimp. "But he's on holiday."
"Never mind," called Turtle.
"Just lift me off this root! I'll get
there somehow."

"What's so special about the other side?" yelled Chimp.

"It's a fantastic place!" shouted Turtle.

Chimp zoomed
down a vine.
"Yeah? That
sounds like my
idea of heaven,"
he said.

"Here – I've just remembered.
I've got long hairy arms and
legs! Point the way, Turtle."
And Chimp swung Turtle to the
other side of the jungle.

"Right," said Chimp, "where is
this fantastic place?"

"What's your idea of heaven,
Chimp?" asked Turtle.
Chimp scratched his head.

Trees for building nests on.
Trees with branches on.
Trees with bits of blue sky poking through.
Trees with ..."

"Mmmm," said Turtle. "Let me think. Got it, Chimp!"

"Look behind you, Chimp.
And left. And right. What do you
see, Chimp?"

Trees?

"Chimp! You've found it!" cried
Turtle.
"Yeah! Just you wait till I tell my
brother. Thanks Turtle!"

And Turtle tottered on ...

... just as Elephant was getting to her feet ... and Cheetah met up with her.

"Have you seen a tricky little turtle anywhere?" asked Cheetah.

"I certainly have," said Elephant.

Let's get him.

But Turtle still had a long way
to go.
Way across the swamp.

"You won't get far," cackled
Crane. "If the snakes don't get
you, the crocs will!"
"What a shame!" said Turtle.

"There's this fantastic place Old Frog told me about. It has everything you could want."

"What? Things to gobble down? Lovely slimy things? Like snakes and ... FROGS? Ha, Ha!"

"Yep!" said Turtle.

"That sounds like heaven," said Crane.

"If only I could fly," sighed crafty Turtle.

"I could fly you," said Crane.

"OK," smiled Turtle.

And Crane flew Turtle across ...

... just as Cheetah and Elephant reached the swamp.

"Land on that big rock!" shouted Turtle.
"Where is it, then?" snapped Crane as soon as they landed.

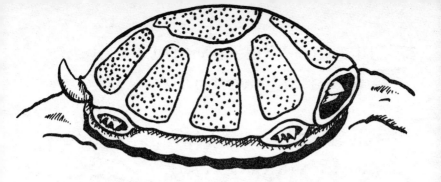

"I'm trying to remember what Old Frog said," yawned Turtle, disappearing into his shell.
"Hurry up! It's getting dark!" said Crane.

But the only sounds were Turtle's snores.

"Just you wait!" she shrieked.
But it was Crane who waited. All
night .
Till next morning when Cheetah
and Elephant arrived.

"There he is!" cried Elephant.
"There's that tricky little
Turtle!"
"He won't trick me again!"
snapped Crane.

"He won't trick anyone again," snarled Cheetah. "Because we've come to get him!"
"All the way over the mountain," said Cheetah.

"And round the swamp," said
Elephant.

"Do you hear, Turtle?" shouted
Cheetah.
"This time you're really going to
get it. Crunch! Crack!
I'm going to bite you in two!
Right down your tricky back!"

"You hear us?" they cried.
"I hear you!" answered a tiny
voice from inside Turtle's shell.
"I deserve it. I'm sorry!
Bite me in two.
Grind me into the rock.
Eat my tail for breakfast
and my toes for tea ...

but whatever you do, PLEASE,
PLEASE, PLEASE ...
don't throw me into the water!"

"Water? What water?" they
cried.
"The horrible deep watery river
below this rock!" sobbed Turtle.

They peered down at the watery
river below.

And Elephant looked at Crane.
And Crane looked at Cheetah.
And Cheetah looked at
Elephant.

Then Elephant curled her trunk round Turtle's shell and they all ran down to the river.

And Elephant hurled Turtle into the most horribly watery part of the river.

Turtle sank like a stone.

As Turtle sank he smiled.

He smiled as he dived.

He smiled as he paddled.

He smiled as he swam, in circles, towards the others.

Turtle was right. It had everything they could ever want. But they were too busy to answer.

Turtle had tricked them all.
But it was worth it!